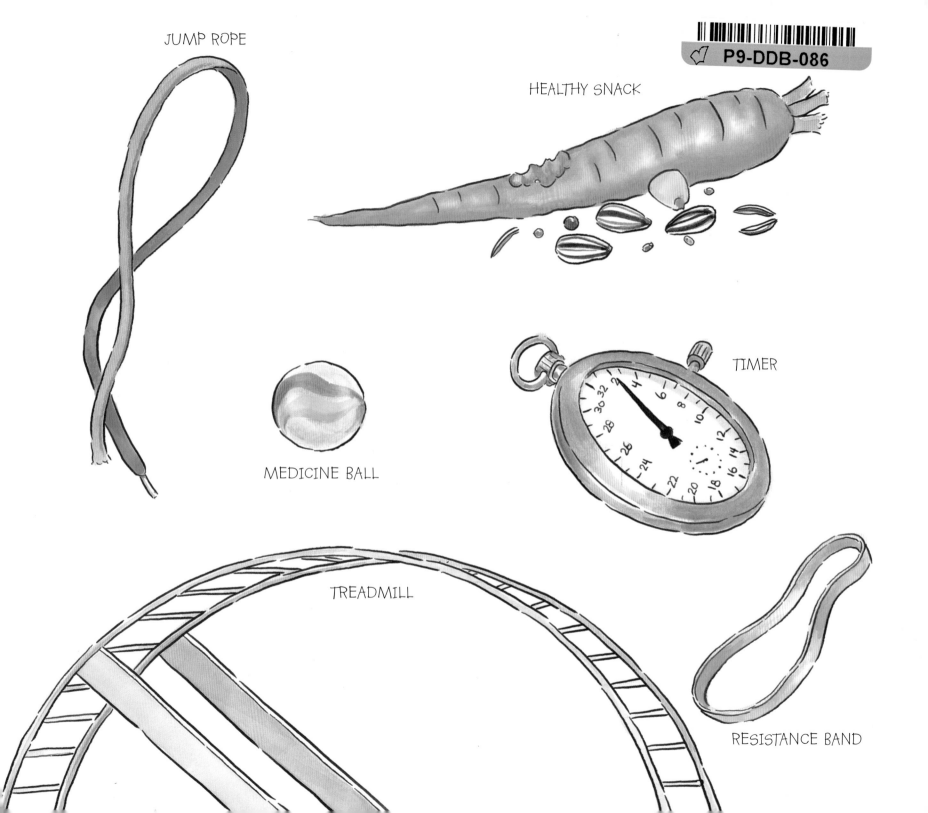

JUMP ROPE

HEALTHY SNACK

TIMER

MEDICINE BALL

TREADMILL

RESISTANCE BAND

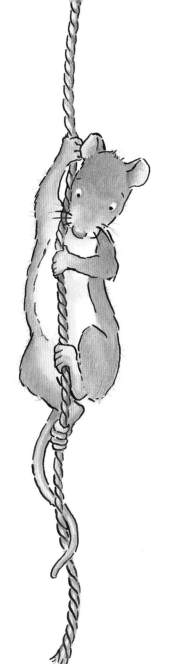

I.Q. Gets Fit

Mary Ann Fraser

Walker & Company
New York

First published in the United States of America in 2007 by
Walker Publishing Company, Inc.
Distributed to the trade by Holtzbrinck Publishers

For information about permission to reproduce selections from
this book, write to Permissions, Walker & Company,
104 Fifth Avenue, New York, New York 10011

Library of Congress Cataloging-in-Publication Data
Fraser, Mary Ann.
I.Q. gets fit / Mary Ann Fraser.
p.   cm.
Summary: During Fitness Month, I.Q., the class pet, learns
important lessons about staying healthy as he tries to win a
gold ribbon in the Student Fitness Challenge.
ISBN-13: 978-0-8027-9558-8 • ISBN-10: 0-8027-9558-7 (hardcover)
ISBN-13: 978-0-8027-9559-5 • ISBN-10: 0-8027-9559-5 (reinforced)
[1. Physical fitness—Fiction. 2. Mice—Fiction. 3. Pets—Fiction.
4. Schools—Fiction.]
I. Title.
PZ7.F86455Inw 2006   [E]—dc22   2006019477

The illustrations for this book were created using colored pencil,
gouache, and pen and ink on Strathmore paper.
Typeset in Gill Sans

Visit Walker & Company's Web site at www.walkeryoungreaders.com

Printed in China
2 4 6 8 10 9 7 5 3 1

All papers used by Walker & Company are natural, recyclable products
made from wood grown in well-managed forests. The manufacturing processes
conform to the environmental regulations of the country of origin.

BEFORE

AFTER

TO EMILY EASTON

HEALTH MONTH—FIRST WEEK

"This is Health Month," said Mrs. Furber, the teacher. "This morning we have an exciting assembly for all students. We are going to learn how to get fit."

I.Q. was the class pet . . . though he really wanted to be a student. He decided he would go to the assembly, too.

At the assembly the speaker explained that if you are fit, your entire body feels good, works well, and allows you to do all the things you want to do.

Just then I.Q.'s stomach made a loud gurgling sound. The kids around him giggled and I.Q.'s ears blushed. He had forgotten to eat breakfast.

"At the end of the month I will come back for the Student Fitness Challenge," said the speaker. "Those students who pass the fitness test will receive a gold ribbon."

Right then I.Q. knew he wanted to win a ribbon.

During PE the students practiced for the fitness challenge. Mrs. Jugar, the PE teacher, wrote down their results.

	SIT UPS	LONG JUMP	PULL UPS
BRETT	55	79"	10
KIM	48	56"	4
TIM	41	46"	8
HOLLY	53	54"	9
ALEX	50	55"	8
SALLY	54	49"	7
IAN	56	52"	6
I.Q.	20	8"	1

I.Q. had not done as well as the other students.
He worried he would not be able to win a gold ribbon.

The next day for art class each student made a fitness poster. Alex helped I.Q. by tracing his shape onto a piece of paper. But after that, I.Q. didn't know what to write on his poster.

Just before lunch Mrs. Furber reminded the students that they should eat many different kinds of food. Every day I.Q. ate macaroni and cheese for lunch. When he went to the cafeteria, he decided to try something different—brownies.

After lunch Mrs. Furber said, "The food pyramid shows how much of each type of food you need for a balanced diet."

I.Q. noticed there were no brownies on the pyramid. Maybe that was why he had a stomachache.

I.Q. wrote on his poster, "Eat a balanced diet."

That night he dreamed he won the Student Fitness Challenge, and his award was a giant brownie.

HEALTH MONTH—SECOND WEEK

The second week Mrs. Furber told the class, "If you want to be physically fit, you must be active. Exercise helps make your heart, lungs, and muscles strong. It also makes you flexible."

I.Q. saw Stephanie and Eric comparing muscles.

He looked at his own muscles.
They were disappointing.

I.Q. tried to touch his toes.
That was disappointing, too.

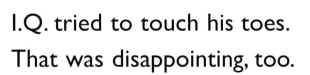

I.Q. really wanted to win a gold ribbon. He made another note on his poster: "Stay active." And he started exercising right away.

That night I.Q. dreamed he had won the gold ribbon, but it weighed too much for him to lift.

In the morning I.Q. could barely get out of bed. Every muscle ached— even the ones in his tail.

On his poster he added a little note: "Warm up and stretch first."

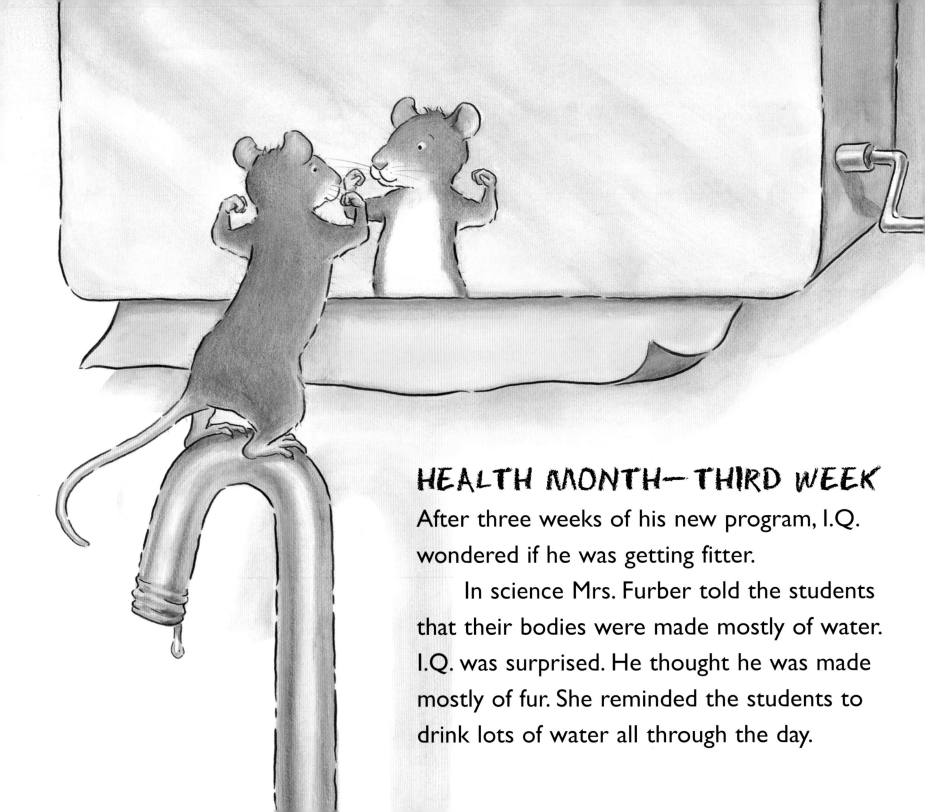

HEALTH MONTH— THIRD WEEK

After three weeks of his new program, I.Q. wondered if he was getting fitter.

In science Mrs. Furber told the students that their bodies were made mostly of water. I.Q. was surprised. He thought he was made mostly of fur. She reminded the students to drink lots of water all through the day.

I.Q. had trouble drinking from the fountain. Fortunately he had a water bottle. On his poster he wrote, "Drink plenty of water."

HEALTH MONTH—FOURTH WEEK

On Monday of the fourth week I.Q. checked out a book from the library. He stayed up very late reading it.

The next day I.Q. fell asleep in the middle of a math problem. Then he tripped and skinned his nose at recess. He had to go to the nurse's office.

When I.Q. got back to class, he realized most of his troubles that day were because he was tired. He finished writing "Get lots of sleep" on his fitness poster just before Mrs. Furber tacked it up with the others.

That night he dreamed he walked in his sleep at the awards ceremony for the Student Fitness Challenge.

A few days later I.Q. checked his poster to make sure he was doing everything right. He was eating well, staying active, drinking plenty of water, and getting enough sleep. Would it be enough to win an award?

On the last day of Health Month each class went to the playground for the Student Fitness Challenge. Everyone was very excited, especially I.Q. As the students did each event, Mrs. Jugar wrote down the results.

I.Q. saw his scores were still lower than everyone else's. His hope for a gold ribbon vanished.

The school gathered for the awards ceremony, and the speaker called the names of the students who had won a ribbon. I.Q. clapped for each one.

Then I.Q. heard his name called. How could he have won a ribbon?

"This is a special ribbon for the student who has improved the most," explained the speaker.

I.Q. was very proud, and he knew just where to keep his ribbon.

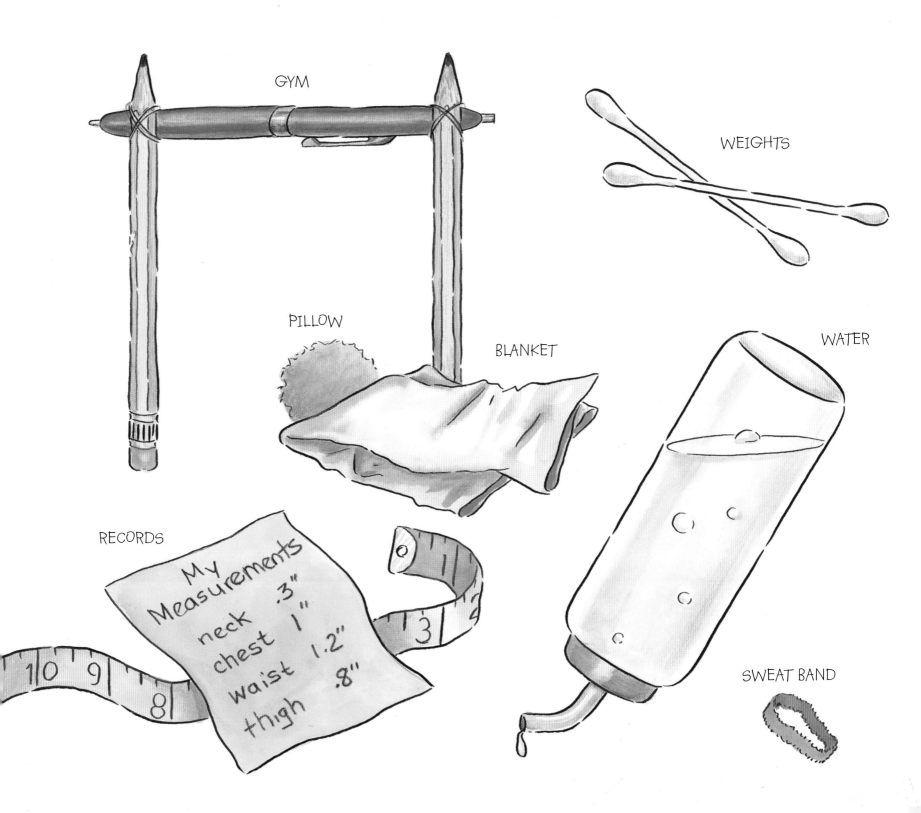

GYM

WEIGHTS

PILLOW

BLANKET

WATER

RECORDS

My
Measurements
neck .3"
chest 1"
waist 1.2"
thigh .8"

SWEAT BAND